A COLORFUL JOURNEY
OUTSIDE THE LINES

HUES
OF HOPE

PRAISE FOR HUES OF HOPE

"A masterful work of art inspiring us all to color again. There are few storytellers who can paint pictures with words the way Will Baggett does. Hope is not a strategy, but it is a necessity."

DARON K. ROBERTS
International Keynote Speaker & Best-Selling Author

"Will Baggett has done it again. 'Hues of Hope' is hard to put down. Through clear, concise, and actionable communication he has crafted an inspiring story for all to never quench the thirst of possibility and discovery. Keep coloring outside the lines is a message that has been timely placed for this current time in our generation. This is an inspiring call to continue coloring outside the realm of possibility."

ED JONES II
Speaker & Founder of Beyond The Field

"'Hues of Hope' serves as a reminder that there's often no preset roadmap for navigating life's twists and turns. It encourages us to chart our own course, much like the explorers of yesteryear who forged new paths as they ventured into the unknown."

D. KELLY BROOKS
Managing Partner, The Brooks Element

"Another wonderful book written by one of my favorite authors. 'Hues of Hope' is a cleverly written easy read that will inspire and motivate the reader. Will Baggett has an uncanny ability to use relatable storytelling to inspire others to greatness!"

ERIC K. SMITH
The Financial Literacy Coach

"'Hues of Hope: A Colorful Journey Outside the Lines' by Will Baggett captivates with its vibrant storytelling and profound life lessons. Baggett masterfully illustrates the power of embracing life's uncertainties, making this a must-read for those seeking hope and inspiration. His unique voice and heartfelt insights mark him as a writer to watch."

MICHAEL S. KELLY
VP & Director of Athletics,
University of South Florida

"Perspective is everything, and optimism can reshape your reality. The nostalgic feeling that brought me back to my southern roots made me smile deep in my heart one moment, while challenging my thoughts and allowing me to fully absorb the profound life lessons presented. The easily digestible nature of 'Hues of Hope' keeps you engaged and leaves you optimistic that YOUR story is the best one yet."

DR. LACEE CARMON-JOHNSON
Keynote Speaker, Manager - Toronto Raptors

"Whether chance encounters or lifelong companions, relationships are what shape us. Author, Will Baggett, shows the power of connection and the perspective that comes from opening your mind to the people you meet along life's journey in his new book 'Hues of Hope'. The opinions of our close friends and family will always carry importance but Baggett carefully constructs the influence of all social ties—long and short— in a powerful and meaningful way."

KELVIN BEACHUM
NFL Veteran & Serial Entrepreneur

Hues of Hope will take you on a chaos theory journey of how life's encounters and circumstances impact not only our outcomes but the outcomes of others.

DR. K. JAMIL NORTHCUTT
Founder & CEO, Strategic Transitions Advisors, LLC

"A quick read with lasting impact! 'Hues of Hope' reminds us that there is power in being present – life becomes vibrant when we embrace all that it can teach us, including the people along the journey. Will provides an uplifting experience with empowering lessons that encourage each of us to lean into our own story!"

JESSIE GARDNER
Executive Associate Athletic Director, University of North Texas

"'Hues of Hope' shares timeless life lessons that can relate to anyone. I felt inspired to embrace the unwritten pages of my life and encouraged to embrace everyone I meet along the journey."

MARK TRUMBO
Associate Director, NCAA Leadership Development

"Will's legacy continues with 'Hues of Hope'. I continued to be inspired by Will's ability to remind us of the power each one of us has to build upon our presence and perspectives in life. Will is a living example of someone who has mastered identifying gaps and filling them with impact and authentic connections. Thank you for always...coloring outside the lines! "

SABLE LEE
Leadership Coach & Consultant, CEO
Courageous Connections

"'Hues of Hope' is an inspirational story that encourages and empowers all of us to have a growth mindset in any situation. No matter where you are in life, this is a great book to read!"

LAMARR POTTINGER
Director, NCAA Leadership Development

"Hope looks different for everyone, it comes in all different sizes, shapes and colors. I'm hopeful that 'Hues of Hope' will do just that, deliver hope. Salute my brother Will for being a hope liver, hope giver, and hope dealer when the world needs it the most."

DERRICK FURLOW JR.
Speaker, Author, and Entrepreneur

"Will is a true transformational servant leader who has inspired me and many others to strive to be our best selves. I've had the opportunity to learn from Will on many different occasions, and it's always been a mindset shifting experience. In the same way, 'Hues of Hope' is yet another life changing deposit into my life."

DERRICK MITCHELL
Athlete Development Professional

"In 'Hues of Hope', Will Baggett guides us through a journey of trials and triumphs, while bridging the gap between personal growth and development. In a time where many people are trying to find their way in life, Baggett provides us with a must-read that leads us out of our comfort zone and encourages us to seek experiences beyond that of what we already know."

ALEXANDER MARTIN
Director of Player Engagement, Miami Dolphins

"In 'Hues of Hope', Will lets us know there is always an opportunity to learn and grow from anyone you encounter. He shows us that if you remain present with an open heart, everything is an opportunity. Will also shows us that in many ways, you don't know where your connections in life begin and end. Will shows that unknown connections, being open to opportunities in spite of difficulties, can be possible even if you're a dollar short."

S. DWAYNE CLARKE
Human Resources Executive

"We are so proud of you, son."

MAGGIE BAGGETT
Mom

"That's my boy."

BILL BAGGETT
Dad

A COLORFUL JOURNEY OUTSIDE THE LINES

HUES OF HOPE

WILL BAGGETT

Inspired by true life events

Hues of Hope: A Colorful Journey Outside the Lines.
First Edition.

Copyright © 2024 by Will Baggett. All rights reserved.

No part of this book may be used or reproduced in any manner whatsoever without written permission except in the case of brief quotations embodied in critical articles or reviews. For more information, email will@execimage.org.

Books may be purchased in bulk for custom editions, gifts, events, or teams. Please email will@execimage.org or visit https://willbaggett.com for additional information.

Cover Design: FaithNiyi Designs
Manuscript Layout: Red Sofa Designs, Inc.
Proofreader: Dorothy Watson

ISBN: 979-8-9909176-0-6

Live life to the fullest.

You have to color outside the lines once in a while if you want to make your life a masterpiece.

Laugh some every day. Keep growing, keep dreaming, keep following your heart.

The important thing is not to stop questioning.

ALBERT EINSTEIN

*For my late friend Anthony Mayes,
who emphasized the importance of
making a "big play" every day of your life.*

CONTENTS

Chapter 1 1

Chapter 2...8

Chapter 3...11

Chapter 4 20

Chapter 5... 23

Chapter 6 31

Chapter 7... 35

Chapter 8...40

Chapter 9 44

Chapter 10...51

Chapter 11...56

Chapter 12..65

CHAPTER 1

"Abraham! Oh, Abraham! Time to get up for school!" yelled Mrs. Wright.

Deafening silence ensued.

Abraham rolled over from one side to the other, opening one eye as he squinted at the sun shining through his uneven blinds. He rolled back over away from the sun, groaned and pulled the covers over his head.

"Abraham! I know you hear me calling your name."

He let out a loud groan.

She was right, but he wasn't ready to get up yet. He'd spent the better part of the night playing Xbox and was already planning to do it over again after school.

Just five more minutes he thought, as he buried his head in his lifeless pillow.

Just then he heard a knock on the door. His mom never came upstairs, so he already knew who it was.

Pops.

"Alright, boy, time to get up," said Pops, and he knew there would be no debate.

"Aight Pops, I'm up, I'm up," Abe grunted. He could faintly hear the creak of the third step from the top of the staircase and knew his dad had begun his descent back downstairs.

It would be his first day as a senior in high school, and he was none too excited about it.

Abe rolled out of bed and proceeded to the closet to get dressed. He didn't make his bed. He never made his bed.

After donning his wrinkled school uniform, he walked over to the window and peaked through one side of the uneven blinds.

The school bus was just two houses away and quickly approaching, yet ever so slowly. He only had one shoe on and had not put his belt on yet.

He slipped on his other all-white Reebok Classic sneaker and darted for his bedroom door, only making it to the creaky third step before tumbling and falling down two steps with a loud thud.

He looked down to find the culprit, which happened to be his beltless jeans.

"Abraham, was that you? Are you alright up there, honey?" Mrs. Wright said. "I think I hear the school bus coming."

"Cuh-cuh coming!" he managed to stutter as he ran back upstairs, half his trousers in tow as he searched frantically for his belt, thrusting clothes and shoes everywhere.

Where is my belt?! He thought.

He knew he would be better off going back to sleep rather than attempting to leave the house without a belt on.

Pops didn't play that.

"Hey son, hurry down here so you can catch that yella helper," said Pops.

That yella what? Who says that? My dad is such a country bumpkin, Abe said to himself.

He then heard a loud screech from outside as the bus came to a halt just one house away. His eyes set upon the swirl of sheets and covers perched upon his unmade bed.

It was the only place he had not looked, so he dove in. He instantly heard a clinking sound, thinking he was getting warmer. Drat.

Just the fifty cents that had fallen out of his pocket the day before. Today's per diem had just been deposited.

Screeeeecch. "Bruhhh, it's almost here. They must have hired a NASCAR driver to replace Mr. Covington," he groaned. Mr. Covington had just retired after 40 years of driving the bus.

"I hear that yella helper out there, boy!" Pops called up from below.

Abe was scrambling. As he peeled back the far end of the comforter, he saw the glimmer of his belt buckle and whipped it on, but not before accidentally hitting himself, leaving a bruise on his left thigh.

Ouch! Without any time to spare, he dashed from his room and down the stairs to try and catch the "yella helper", or whatever Pops called it.

Pops had just left for work, but Mom was still downstairs in the kitchen. With his half-zipped backpack swinging from one arm, he kissed his mom on the cheek and dashed outside.

The screech from the school bus's brakes could only be heard in the distance by now as the bus made its way down the road.

He could just make out the numbers 6-4 on the back door as he saw the Chaney twins going up the bus steps four houses down. "There goes the neighborhood," Abe sulked.

He walked back into the house to the warm gaze of his mother. "Is the bus gone?" she asked.

"Yeah, I missed it,'' Abe replied reluctantly as he swung his backpack to the ground and plopped down at the kitchen table.

His mom, sensing his frustration, slipped something in her apron unbeknownst to Abe and walked over to help. "Some way to start off my senior year, huh?" said Abe.

"Oh, it's okay. Now you have time to eat breakfast!" his mom quipped.

"But how am I going to get to school? Isn't your car still in the shop?"

"Oh, don't worry about that, you can catch the city bus. It stops about a block away from the school."

"The one with the crazy bus driver lady?! Uh no, I'd rather walk. She's too bubbly for me and always calls me "sugar".

Abe stood up to make his point. "And I heard she has a bunch of rules on that bus, too."

"Now Abe, that's not very nice. Ms. Gurt is a sweet lady and prides herself on never having met a stranger."

"I mean, I would think not. If she's one thing, she's strange," he quipped as he took a seat at the kitchen table.

"Now Abraham, what does it say in the Good Book about strangers. Remember?" his mom quipped.

Abe thought for a moment, "Something about being careful not to ignore strangers because you could be around an angel or something like that."

"Exactly!" his mom said proudly. "Anywho, I suggest you take a seat and be sure you clean this table when you finish eating. You'd better hurry so you don't miss another bus, dear."

With that, it was settled. His mom was a sweet, gentle spirit, but always meant what she said.

All he could do was smile as he upended his bowl to gulp the leftover milk from his Frosted Flakes.

CHAPTER 2

The first segment of the local news was nearing its end, so he knew he'd better get going.

He could overhear Frank Nettles, the sports anchor, wrapping up some story about college football in the living room as he stood up.

"Thanks, mama," Abe called out to his mom as he zipped his backpack and started for the door.

"Um, didn't you forget something?" she said.

Abe knew what she was talking about deep down, but he didn't like all the mushy stuff. "Where's my hug?"

"Okay, okay," he muttered as he trudged back to her. Abe's mom had been injured in a car wreck a year earlier and was unable to work. He had no clue how she managed to stay so positive despite her condition.

As his mom wrapped her arms around him, he could only begin to think about the small stuff from this morning that he allowed to get him down.

Yet, here was his mom, who despite her condition, made a daily decision to be joyful.

"Now Abe, remember that you can't always control what happens to you, but you can control your response. I know today didn't begin the way you wanted it to, but that doesn't mean it can't end well."

"Yeah, you're always right. I just feel like it's been a day already, and it's not even eight o'clock," Abe said as he massaged what was now a small welt on his left thigh.

"Oh I'm sure it has been. I heard that loud thud you made this morning and couldn't help but laugh on the inside," she giggled, "and outside."

"Yeah, yeah, yeah. Can't hold me down for long though. I'm about to see if I can catch that other bus," he said smugly.

"You know what your dad always says: A poor ride is better than a proud walk," she quipped.

Great. Another Pop-ism. Abe gave her the side-eye knowing she'd got him again, only to find that his mom had already begun her victory lap skipping around the house.

"Have a good day, son! I love you!" she said in her sing-song voice, "Let's shoot the hoop when you get home this evening!"

Guess she wants to get these buckets after school, Abe muttered to himself with a smirk.

"You don't want none!" Abe called back to her on his way out.

He gave her a preview of what was to come by yelling "Kobe!" as he canned his breakfast napkin from all of three feet out.

With that, he pulled on his headphones and marched down the front steps toward the bus stop.

CHAPTER 3

As he neared the bus station, and saw the bus rates, he checked his pockets to make sure he had enough money for a one-way trip.

The sign read $2.50 per trip.

Shaking his pockets for dear life, he found the fifty cents from this morning.

I can't even get a piggyback ride for that kind of money, he thought.

Abe patted himself down like a TSA agent and found a crumpled dollar bill in his back pocket. He now had $1.50 to his name but was still a day late and a dollar short of the $2.50 bus fare.

This is not happening, he thought. Pops is going to kill me if he gets a phone call saying that I'm skipping school.

He sat down on the curb and put his head in his hands.

Just as he was about to begin the walk back home, the city bus pulled up and Ms. Gurt appeared behind the folded glass doors.

"Lil Wright, is that you? Hay! Boy, I haven't seen you since you were knee-high to a grasshopper. How is your mama 'nem doing, Sugar?"

She definitely came up in the same era as Pops, he thought. Where do they come up with this stuff?

"Hey there, Ms. Gurt. Yes'm, they are doing good."

"Hay! It's a great day with Gurt! That's what I like to hear," she said as she flashed her signature smile revealing the glint of her gold tooth. "Need a ride?"

"Yes'm, but I'm short on funds and only have $1.50 to my name. I'm busted and can't be trusted. Plus, I missed the school bus this morning."

"Them yella helpers ain't good for much of nothing. They're either too early or too late, and speed up when they see ya coming."

"Oh no, not you too," Abe muttered to himself.

"But hay!," she said with a clap. "You're good people, and I know your folks, so come along and ride on Ms. Gurt's bus! I knew your granddaddy Reverend Wright too, ya know."

Abe's grandfather passed away when he was just a baby.

"Really? You're going to let me ride for free?"

"Of course not. Come on off that $1.50, and we'll call it even. Hay! Ms. Gurt's gotta eat too now. Now come along and ride on this fantastic voyage!" she joked as her gold tooth sparkled in the sun.

Abe smiled as he emptied his pockets, lint and all, into the receptacle. He placed his headphones back on his ears and proceeded past the other passengers to find an empty seat.

"Uh uh, Lil Wright. No Walkman's allowed when you're burning Ms. Gurt's gas."

"What's a Walkman?" asked Abe.

"You're gonna be a walking man and not a riding man if you don't put those headphones up. Now are you picking up what Ms. Gurt's putting down?"

"Yes, ma'am," Abe uttered under his breath.

"Back in my day we used to talk to people. Do that. Talk to somebody. Seems like people are so connected that they're disconnected these days."

She had a point.

Abe took a seat on an empty row of two seats, opting for the one nearest to the window.

By this time, Ms. Gurt had begun a conversation with one of her regulars.

This was his chance. He slumped down into the seat, put his headphones back on, buried his head into the seatback in front of him.

Ms. Gurt's bus continued through the city, ignoring every speed bump and yield sign it encountered along the way.

Moments later, the bus stopped for current passengers to get off and new passengers to get on.

Abe kept his face planted into the seat in front of him and began to doze off.

Moments later, a bald-headed, squirrely man sat down beside him. He had rounded spectacles, suspenders, and was holding a brown-looking book staring straight ahead.

He was dressed casually and didn't appear to be in a rush to get anywhere in particular. Abe glanced at the book on his lap. It had a very unique cover.

Abe leaned over a little as the man gazed forward in hopes of making out the words printed on the cover, but they were mostly faded out.

Even over the pulsating rhythms echoing through his Beats headphones, Abe could still hear Ms. Gurt's unmistakable cackle.

They were passing through a nice neighborhood that was going through gentrification, so some houses were worn down while others were newly developed.

Must be nice to live in an area like this, he thought to himself.

"I'm gonna get me one of these spots one day," he declared under his breath.

"Pardon?" said the squirrely man with lowered glasses.

Abe slid back his headphones from his ears, but held on to the sides in an effort to put them right back on. "Oh nothing, sir, sorry. I was just talking to myself."

"Aha! Quite alright, my good man. As long as you don't answer yourself, you're in good shape, lad," he countered.

Abe couldn't suppress a laugh. "I don't think it's gotten that bad yet, but I'll let ya know if it does."

"What is your forename, my good man?"

"Oh, I'm Abe. Nice to meet you, Mr.----?"

"Short for Abraham, I presume? Aha! But Abe it is if you insist, lad. I go by Mackson, my good man."

Abe raised out of his seat slightly only to be shortened a few inches after bumping his head on the overcarriage. "Ow! Do you know where we are?"

Mackson stared out of the window nostalgically. "Everywhere but nowhere my man. The best place to be. Once you know where you're going, you begin to appreciate the journey itself much, much more."

Abe looked at him with a thoughtful expression of confusion. He wanted to ask a question, but didn't know how to frame it.

The bus came to a screeching halt, and passengers slowly rose to their feet and began filing out one by one.

Abe checked his watch. 7:47 a.m.

He had to be at school by 8 a.m. and wasn't exactly sure how far of a walk it was, but before he could even ask, Ms. Gurt chimed in.

"Trying to get to the schoolhouse, baby? Head on up 45th Street, make a left by the park and it's a straight shot from there. Bout a ten-or-eleven-minute walk."

Geez, I'm going to be cutting it close, Abe thought.

"Hay! Well, you better get to step-steppin', Sugar!" Ms. Gurt said with a clap and a smile. Her gold tooth caught the ray of the sun again, nearly blinding him.

"And act like you have been somewhere before and get yourself together. Your packbag is open and so is your fly!"

My what?

She walked over to help him with his backpack while he took care of the front of house operations.

"Hay! Alright now!" she said with a clap. "You're ret to go now!"

Abe thanked her, adjusted his headphones and started for school. He passed all the other bus drivers standing outside waiting on their next set of passengers.

Even as he turned onto 45th Street, he could still smell the exhaust from the buses.

He passed by a few blocks and until he reached the park where he was supposed to make a left, according to Ms. Gurt. There were a few small children playing on the swings and merry-go-round.

There were also a few people meandering through the park. He marched on swiftly.

It was 7:58 a.m.

CHAPTER 4

He had a couple of minutes to spare, so he cut around the cafeteria to an area where his basketball buddies usually hung out. As he rounded the corner, he saw them outside talking, so he greeted them with a handshake.

"Why are you sweating, bro?" Jay asked.

"Yeah bro, long night or short morning?" Mike chipped in. He was the jokester of the crew and always had something to say.

Abe couldn't help but smile as he gave them both a light shove. "Man, all of the above and then some. I missed the school bus this morning and had to ride the city bus with Ms. Gurt."

"Ahh man, I've heard about her, bro. Is she as creepy as people say she is?" said Jay.

Abe smirked. "Eh, she's not that bad, just old school."

The bell rang right on cue at 8:00 a.m. Jay and Cam dapped Abe up before heading to their first period class the two shared.

Abe went his way as he entered the building and headed to his math class.

It wasn't his favorite subject, but Mr. Larinde was cool and did everything he could to make it fun. He went to his usual seat on the second row and unzipped his backpack to grab his books.

As he reached into his backpack and felt around, his fingers grazed an unusual, grainy texture. It felt like a book or something. He yanked it out with curiosity and set it on his desk.

It was eerily similar to the faded brown book the guy on the bus was holding! He looked closely to try and make out the words on the front cover.

Something something something...Lines, it read.

He could not make out the other words in the title as they were illegible, but he opened it in hopes of figuring out what it was about.

Odd. The first page was blank. But so was the second and third page. He kept flipping through.

They were all blank.

"Is this some sort of joke?" Abe said to himself. "Who would carry around a book this long with no words in it?"

He slid the mystery book back into his backpack with a shrug and prepared himself for the day's trigonometry lesson. All he could think about was taking the city bus home and asking the guy with the accent about the book.

CHAPTER 5

Bell sounds

At last. Sixth period. Abe was a great student, and his parents made it clear that academics were a non-negotiable if he wanted to stay on the basketball team.

Abe entered the gym where he found Jay and Cam already putting shots up. He proceeded into the locker room to suit up before Coach Hutchinson blew the whistle for practice to start.

It was a long one, but practice ended a few minutes before the period was over. Abe got dressed and headed over to his 7th period English class to finish up the day.

They had a substitute teacher on the first day, which was good.

He'd heard the regular teacher was a real weirdo, and the day had already been weird enough.

He opened up his backpack to find his notebook, and remembered the mystery book he had been carrying around all day.

He pulled out the faded, brown book and flipped through the empty pages. He didn't pay it any attention at first, but he noticed the pages didn't even have lines to keep your words straight.

Some book he thought, and closed it with frustration. I'll just have to make do with what I have, he decided, as the substitute teacher opened up saying something about poetry. Something like that.

As soon as the seventh period ended, he charged outside to try and make it to the city bus stop before Ms. Gurt left. Cam had paid him the five bucks he owed him, so he was in good shape funds wise.

Abe made it just in time as she was closing the doors.

As he ascended the steps, he reached into his pocket for the crumbled up five-dollar bill Cam had given him and handed it to Ms. Gurt.

"Well, hay! How many coins have you got for Ms. Gurt this evening, baby?!" The glint of her gold tooth gleaming in the evening sun.

"I got $2.50 plus interest, plus my debt from earlier today. Paid in full," Abe said with pride.

"Well hand it over, baby, and come along and ride on this fantastic voyage!"

That sounds like one of the oldie songs my dad plays, Abe thought with a slight grin. I wonder if she says that every day, shaking his head as he proceeds past Ms. Gurt.

He started down the aisle hoping to see his new friend, but he was nowhere to be seen. He turned around.

"Hey Ms. Gurt, does Mr. Mackson ride the bus in the evening?"

"Who?" she replied.

"You know, Mackson, the guy with the round glasses who talks funny."

"Baby, Ms. Gurt knows everybody on her bus, and I ain't never heard of no Mackson, whatchamacallit," she called back.

Confused, Abe took an aisle seat near the center of the bus as it continued on its way.

"Don't be doing all that snoring and carrying on like you were this morning, now. You were louder than Ms. Gurt's engine."

Then it hit him. He had been dreaming.

He unzipped his backpack and shuffled through it frantically. Sure enough, there it was. He turned the book over in his hands, trying to make sense out of what had transpired since that morning.

"So where did this empty book come from then?" he muttered to himself.

As they weaved through the surrounding neighborhoods, Abe couldn't help but think about his dream as he clasped the book in his hands.

It seemed so real.

"What are you reading back there, Lil Wright? You know Ms. Gurt likes her stories. Ooh wee, is it like 'Days of our Lives'?"

"I have no idea what you are talking about, Ms. Gurt. But honestly, I don't know what the book is about. There are no words on the pages."

He flipped through it once more, "It's completely empty, see."

Ms. Gurt glanced through her overhead mirror.

"Sounds like a best seller to me," said Ms. Gurt with a wink.

"What do you mean?"

"Listen, whoever gave you that book knows a lot," she explained.

Raising his eyebrow, Abe thought to himself, "That makes zero sense."

"Now Ms. Gurt may joke a lot but she'd been around the block before she became a bus driver. And this is what I will tell you, no one has your fingerprint, so no one can make your imprint. Hay! Is Ms. Gurt right? Yes, or yes?"

"I mean, I guess, but what does that mean exactly?" Abe asked.

"It means that he who controls the printed page controls the thinking of the age! Hay!" she quipped.

"Now, more than ever, I see young people trying to be a secondhand version of someone else instead of a firsthand version of themselves."

"Yeah, I can see that."

"Hey, let Ms. Gurt tell you a little something that I learned about being a bus driver after all these years. No one knows exactly what they are doing. You're gonna be in a lot of important places with a lot of average people."

"Really? I've always thought people were so much smarter and better than I am," said Abe.

"Hay now! Everyone is a genius, but if you judge a fish by its ability to climb a tree, it will spend the rest of its life thinking it's a dummy. Is Ms. Gurt right? Yes or yes?"

"Yeah, I guess you are. Thanks for that, Ms. Gurt."

"You're welcome! Hay! Always remember that when you are being rejected, you are being redirected. Just think about it. If you had not missed that yella helper, you would not have met Ms. Gurt!"

"That's fair. This is definitely more entertaining than the school bus," Abe said slyly.

"Well, let Ms. Gurt lay something on ya. If you ride with me for the rest of the week, I will tell you everything I know about life, and we gone fill up them pages in the book. How's that sound?"

"You've got a deal Ms. Gurt!" Abe said.

The bus continued on its route as passengers exited at their stops, before rounding the corner and stopping at Abe's drop point.

"Alright, baby. Ms. Gurt has got to go watch her stories," she clapped, "So let's get you on your way home."

Abe couldn't help but smile as he rose from his seat and headed for the exit, hugging Ms. Gurt on his way out.

"Thanks for the ride, Ms. Gurt!" Abe called out.

With a clap and a cackle, Ms. Gurt replied, "Hay! It's all good in the neighborhood, baby! Have a good day now, ya hear!"

CHAPTER 6

Abe began his trek inside the house where his parents were waiting. As he walked inside, there was his mom greeting him with her warm smile.

"How was your first day?" she rang out.

"Um, it was a day. That's for sure."

Just then, he heard the door close behind him as Pops was walking in from work. He set his hat down on the table and greeted his mom with a kiss on the cheek before addressing Abe.

"Hey there boy, did you have a good day? You make it on that yella helper this morning?"

"Not exactly. I made it on a helper, but it wasn't exactly 'yella'. More of a faded green color, but it got the job done."

"Alright, alright. I hear ya. Wait, turn around. Did you miss a belt loop? Looks like a couple of 'em, matter of fact."

Abe looked down and sure enough one side of his pants was hanging lower than the other. He couldn't believe he'd been walking around like this all day and hadn't noticed. He unbuckled his belt to try and fix it.

"Sorry, Pops. I know you don't like me leaving the house without a belt, so I rushed to put one on this morning."

"It's okay, son. I understand, but always remember what I told you. Be quick, but don't hurry. When you're in a hurry, you don't think straight. And that dog won't hunt."

Abe couldn't hold back a smile after that Pop-ism. "Yeah, I know, Pops. I'll keep that in mind and do better next time."

"That's my boy."

With that, he gave Abe a light hug and told him to go get settled. Abe proceeded upstairs into his room knowing the mess that awaited him. The first thing he noticed was his unmade bed that looked like it had been hit by a tornado.

He then turned his attention to his uneven blinds that were literally hanging on by a thread. There was a paper plate with sandwich crumbs on his dresser, clothes that needed to be folded and shoes everywhere.

He unloaded his backpack and whipped off his belt from the few loops that were occupied. It came off quicker than he expected, but he was careful not to reaggravate the self-inflicted wound he'd given himself earlier that morning.

He sat on the edge of his bed to unwind and think about all that had occurred since he left this very spot the same morning. A missed bus. An unforgettable driver. A very realistic dream. And an empty...

Just then he remembered the wordless book in his backpack, and grabbed it to flip through again.

It had to be old considering how the cover looked and some of the binding was coming apart. But not so old that they could not have printed something inside of it, he thought.

He flipped through it again, and of course, he found nothing.

That was until he flipped to the very last page. Just barely legible in the bottom right corner were these words:

> *Everything I know about life is captured in the preceding pages.*
> –FRED M. WRIGHT

Thinking he'd missed something, he flipped back through the rest of the book.

Clear as kleenex.

Seconds later, he heard a knock on the door. "May I come in?" It was his mom.

Scrambling to hide the book, he managed to call out, "Sure, it's open," Abe said.

"Did you find the present I left in your backpack this morning," his mom said with a warm smile. "It belonged to your grandfather."

CHAPTER 7

The next morning, Abe woke up from his sleep before his alarm clock sounded.

With one eye open, he looked over at his phone to check the time, and quickly realized he was 30 minutes ahead of schedule.

"That's a first," he said as he wiped the sleep from his eyes.

By this time, his sheets were hanging on for dear life on three of four corners. Determined not to miss the school bus again, he swung himself out of bed.

He carefully pulled his pants on and made sure to lace his belt through each loop this time. Just as he was reaching for his shirt, he heard a slow creaking of the staircase and knew it had to be Pops on his way up.

Before he could get halfway up, Abe called out, "I'm up, Pops!"

"Alright now, pay your fare and comb your hair!" he said rhythmically.

With an eye roll and a light smile, Abe called down, "Yeah, yeah, yeah. I hear ya."

Abe continued to get dressed in the jungle that was his bedroom, occasionally tripping over a sneaker here and there. He looked out of the tangled blinds to make sure the bus wasn't coming.

He then grabbed a pullover he was sure he hadn't worn in at least three days to complete the outfit for the day.

He looked down at his half-zipped backpack to make sure he had everything he needed. Belt. Textbooks. iPad. Notebook Check. Check. Check. Check.

He then recalled the one thing that was "missing". The empty book. He sifted through his covers until he found it, slid it into his backpack and made his way downstairs where Pops was hanging out in the kitchen.

His mom had already left for the beauty shop, so he wouldn't be able to ask her about the empty book.

Pop checked his watch. "You're mighty early today. Guess you're not trying to miss that yella helper again this morning," he said slyly.

Abe thought about how he would respond and then quipped, "I think I'm going to ride with Ms. Gurt again today. It was kinda fun."

Pops nearly spit out his coffee. "Come again?" he said.

"Something wrong with that yella helper?" Pops continued.

"Oh no, everything is fine. I just thought it would be cool to go off the beaten path again today."

"Well, do you have any greenbacks for the bus?"

Abe shot back a puzzled look.

"Greenbacks. Money. Cold hard cash, son," his Pops shot back.

"That, I do not," Abe admitted as he pulled out the insides of his pockets. "All donations are welcomed though!"

Pops reached into his pocket, pulled out a five-dollar bill and handed it to Abe. "Here you go, son. Don't spend it all in one place."

Just then they heard a loud screeching sound from down the street and knew the school bus was approaching.

"Sure you don't need help from that yella helper?" his Pops called out.

With a bite of his bacon, Abe stood up and shook his head, "Nope."

He then went over to the window to watch as the school bus approached. The bus driver stopped right in front of Abe's house.

Mr. Covington opened the folding doors, looked around to see if anyone was in sight, then with a shake of his head closed the door and proceeded down the street to pick up the Chaney twins.

Once the school bus was out of sight, Abe waved goodbye to his dad and set out toward the bus stop.

The school day dragged on for Abe, primarily because his focus just wasn't on his "lesson" as Ms. Gurt and

Pops liked to say. He really wanted to ask his mom about his grandfather's blank book.

The bell rang.

"Sixth period baby!" Abe called out as he entered the hallway. He was running down the hall on his way to the gym, when he heard someone call out from behind him.

"Tuck in your shirt."

He turned to find Mrs. Leverette, his actual English teacher who'd been absent the day before, standing in the doorway sneering at him.

She was wearing a custom denim jacket, covered in red apple stitchings. She also had one of those chains attached to her speckled glasses so she never lost them. There wasn't a hair strand out of place on her head.

He faked a smile and obliged as she reentered her classroom.

"I'll see you in 7th perioddd," Mrs. Leverette sang out from inside. It echoed across the hallway.

Terrified, he proceeded to the gym.

CHAPTER 8

Practice ended, Abe got dressed, and proceeded to his 7th period class with Mrs. Leverette. He dreaded every step toward his destination not knowing what awaited him.

He took his precious time, stopping at every water fountain he passed and talking to every friend who was within earshot.

His goal was to arrive at class as close to the bell ringing as possible, and he was on schedule, if you will.

Finally, the moment of truth had come. He'd heard Mrs. Leverette was very strict and in some ways mean, so he wasn't looking forward to spending his senior year in her classroom.

Walking in, he found a seat in the middle near the back of the room.

The bell rang.

He looked around, and it appeared that everyone else had heard the same stories about Mrs. Leverette as he had.

Based on the smug look on her face, Mrs. Leverette appeared to be aware of the folklore that preceded her.

Embracing it, even, as she rose from her desk. She turned around to grab something propped up in the corner, but no one could make out what it was.

In an instant, she whipped out a broomstick with a horse puppet on top of it.

She then mounted it, and galloped around the classroom!

The entire classroom was in a state of shock as she gleefully galloped around the perimeter of the class, laughing hysterically with each stride.

After what seemed like an eternity, she completed her ride at the front of the classroom and dismounted her trusty steed.

She carefully scanned the room, looking every person in their eyes.

She then said, "You all probably think I'm crazy, don't you?"

There was an ever-so-slight collective nod across the room.

"Well, don't just sit there. Write about it," Mrs. Leverette said with a clap and a cackle.

She continued, "This is your first assignment, and it will be graded."

Confused, Abe looked around to see if anyone was mortified as he was, but they had already taken out paper and began writing.

Following suit, he reached into his backpack for his notebook, but it was nowhere to be found.

"Shoot," he thought, "I must have left it in the gym."

So he rummaged through the rest of the contents and found the blank book that belonged to his grandfather, and opened it to the second to last page to tear out a sheet of paper.

Unable to yank out a sheet on the first try, he looked down to get a better grip and saw a new entry at the bottom of the page. It was his mom's handwriting.

To Abraham:

You have to color outside the lines once in a while if you want to make your life a masterpiece. Everything won't always fit perfectly onto the page, and that's okay. You aren't bound by anything but your mind.

– Mom

With a smile, he closed the book, slipped it back into his backpack, and asked to borrow a sheet of paper from his classmate.

He began to write.

CHAPTER 9

Rinnnnggggg!

That was the 7th period bell signaling the school day was over.

Abe had been so consumed with his writing that he had to borrow additional sheets from his classmate.

He looked around and noticed a majority of his classmates had already departed. So, he finished up his thought, turned in his paper, and began to pack up.

On his way to the bus stop, he could not help but replay today's events in his mind.

Saying to himself, "Geez, two straight days of weirdness. Is anyone normal these days, or is everyone just going off the deep end these days?"

Moments later, Ms. Gurt pulled up to the bus stop signaling for Abe to come aboard, but her brakes were so bad that he'd heard approaching miles before she arrived.

"Hay! Have no fear, Ms. Gurt is here!" she said with her infamous clap, her gold tooth gleaming as bright as ever.

"I think I'm actually scared now that you're here," Abe muttered under his breath with a smirk.

"Now look-a-here, if you give me lip, you get no trip! A poor ride is better than a proud walk, ya hear?" she shot back.

"Yes'm, I get it. I was just messing with you. I actually like riding your bus nowadays. The seats are much more comfortable," Abe gestured.

"Sho' ya right!," Ms. Gurt agreed. "And let me tell you a little secret about being a bus driver. It's a lot like life."

"How so?" Abe asked.

"If you want to get where you're going, you have to get the right people on the bus and get them in the right seats," said Ms. Gurt.

"I understand getting the right people on the bus, but why does it matter where they sit?" Abe inquired.

"Hay! Because if there's too much weighing down one side of the bus, Ms. Gurt will start swerving in and outside the lines. Now Ms. Gurt don't mind coloring outside the lines, but she don't like driving outside them."

"Wait…driving…coloring…why do I keep hearing about these lines? Like there's this book I got that my mom gave me, but there's no lines, words, or anything in it. What am I supposed to do with that?"

"Write your own story, baby! What else?" Ms. Gurt shot back.

"I guess I never thought about it that way. I was just going to do what everyone else was doing," Abe said nonchalantly.

"Hay! If you do what they do, you gone get what they get. And listen here, this ain't that, and that ain't this! A short pencil is better than a long memory!"

Unable to hide his smile, Abe reached into his backpack to grab the book and make an entry.

> Write your own story.

Shortly after finishing the entry, he peered out of the window and noticed they were nearing the bus stop nearest to his home.

He noticed a man standing by the bench singing melodically as people passed by. It appeared he was down on his luck and was seeking donations.

As Abe descended the bus steps, the singer turned his attention to him and began singing a rendition of "Human Nature" by Michael Jackson.

"Why...why...does he do me that way..." sang the man.

He stopped mid verse to ask Abe for spare change.

"I'm sorry, sir. I only have a few quarters. Will that help?"

"Anything helps," he replied as he took the change from Abe.

"What's your name?" Abe inquired.

Surprised by his interest, the man stood up straight, adjusted his shirt and said, "Voice. Voice Williams."

"So wait, Voice is your real name? That's so cool. And the fact you can sing too—how did your parents know to name you that?"

"Not sure. I just remember her singing to me as a young boy. I had some things not go my way, but I'm trying to use my gift now to make ends meet. I always wanted to sing, but I just did what other people wanted me to do. I was kinda afraid to color outside the lines."

"Wait, can you repeat that? I'm not sure I heard you right," Abe said with disbelief.

"Yeah, I was afraid to color outside the lines. This is who I wanted to be before the experts got involved."

"This is crazy!" Abe said under his breath.

"Nah, what's crazy is that most people just ignore me and walk past. They think I'm homeless. But how can I be homeless in a land where my heavenly Father has dominion over all the land. Everything you see is part of my inheritance."

"Wow, what a perspective." Abe said nearly speechless.

"That's all life is bro...perspective. It's all about how you see things. The problem is never the problem. It's how you respond to it. And I choose joy. Happiness is either where you are right now, or nowhere at all.

A group of seemingly well-off shoppers were approaching, so Voice began warming up his voice again.

"Why...why...tell them that it's human nature...," hummed Voice.

He paused to address Abe, "Welp, back to the grind, my guy. Always remember you build trust by keeping your promises to other people. You build confidence by keeping your promises to yourself.

Abe whipped out the mysterious book and made a new entry.

> You build trust by keeping your promises to other people.
>
> You build confidence when you keep your promises to yourself.

Abe continued on his way home.

Upon entering, he was greeted by his mom in the kitchen as his dad watched wrestling, or as his dad called it, "rasslin".

Abe swung his backpack down and grabbed the formerly empty book from inside.

"So mom, about this book you gave me," Abe quizzed her.

She shot a quick glance at his dad, then to him, and motioned for him to have a seat.

CHAPTER 10

"I put the book in your backpack because I wanted you to stay encouraged. I found the denial letter to the college you wanted to go to," his mom shared.

"Yeah, I tried to keep it kind of a secret. I didn't want to disappoint you and Pops."

"Oh no, you could never do that. Sometimes redirection is just protection in a really good disguise," mom said.

Abe grabbed his book and made a new entry.

His mom smiled as he wrote.

> Sometimes redirection is just protection in a really good disguise.

"I see you're making good use of your new guide," she said.

"Eh, guide is a bit of a stretch don't you think? It's kinda off the beaten path," he quipped.

"Whoever said life had to go in a straight line?" his mom shot back.

"I guess you're right. It's just that granddad's note on the last page didn't make any sense. It said 'everything I know about life is in the preceding pages'."

His mom nodded with a warm smile.

He continued, "But they were all blank. By the way, what was grandpa's middle name?"

Abe's grandfather passed away when he was only a year old.

"It was Mackson. Why do you ask?"

Abe looked up in utter disbelief.

"I think I had a dream about him on the bus. What was he like, mom?"

"Let's just say he moved to his own beat, and was never one for the status quo. He was the first person to publish a book with no words printed on the pages, and you're holding it as we speak."

"Really?" Abe said in disbelief

"Really, really. It became a bestseller even after he was turned away by 46 publishers. They said it was lacking…imagine that," she said with a smile as she stared into the distance.

"But 46, though? He just would not take no for an answer, huh?" Abe inquired.

"Let me show you something, honey."

Abe's mom rose from her chair and went over to the cabinet underneath the kitchen sink as Abe and his dad looked on. She grabbed two items from underneath the sink and walked back over to the table.

"What are those for?" Abe said, puzzled.

Abe's mom set a partially empty can of WD-40 and a bottle of Formula 409 on the table and cut her eyes over at him.

"Do you know the story behind these products, dear," Mom asked.

"Uh, well one is for making things move more smoothly and the other is for cleaning up, so what?"

"That is true, but what you know about these products is their fruit, but not their root. WD-40 stands for "water displacement - 40 attempts", and Formula 409 means the 409th attempt was the one that worked."

"No way. You made that up, mom."

"Yes way, dear. Google it why don't you, and while you there, look up the fact that Google was a misspelling. It was supposed to be spelled G-o-o-g-o-l at first, but they misspelled it and decided to stick with it."

"Wow, I never knew these big companies had all those failures."

"Depends on how you look at it, dear. Did they fail, or did just find a bunch of ways that didn't work. Imagine if they had only colored inside the lines. They would have quit much sooner. Every no makes room for the next opportunity."

With a nod of understanding and a smile, Abe opened his grandfather's bestseller and began to write.

> Whenever you get a 'n-o', that just means next opportunity.

CHAPTER 11

Abe was awakened the next morning by his alarm clock.

Soulja Boy was in the midst of singing:

"Hop up out the bed, turn my swag on..." for the sixth time before Abe reached over and stopped him mid sentence.

Rubbing the sleep from his eyes, he finally got up to turn his swag on which consisted of a wrinkled polo shirt, khaki pants, and a pair of New Balance 574's.

By now, he was used to hearing the screech of Mr. Covington's "yella helper" as it came and went.

What used to be an outright pause in front of his house had become more of a rolling stop of sorts.

Abe was just fine with that.

He grabbed his backpack, careful not to forget his grandfather's book, and headed out for the bus stop.

Ms. Gurt's bus was just turning onto the street where Abe was waiting.

She passed by Abe before coming to a full stop and motioning for him to come and board.

"Hay! If Ms. Gurt had stopped any closer to ya, you woulda smelled what I had for breakfast."

She had gone at least twenty feet past the bus stop marker.

"Is that right? Morning, Ms. Gurt," Abe said with a laugh.

"Don't you sass Ms. Gurt, now. Go on and have a seat. Hay! It's a great day with Gurt!" she said with her famous cackle.

Abe continued down the aisle, passing a number of people. The bus was busy today.

He passed by an older, well-dressed man in a blazer who was busily typing away on his laptop. He did not even notice Abe was approaching as he banged out what sounded like 1,000 words per minute.

Abe continued just past him to an empty row, across the aisle from a little boy and his mom. It appeared his mom had taken the window seat so she could lean against the window and catch up on sleep.

Abe plopped down to occupy one of the two seats in the empty row and buried his head into the seat in front of him.

Moments later, he heard a scratching sound, so he unburied his head and perched up to find the source of the sounds.

It was the little boy.

He could not have been more than five or six, and it appeared he was catching up on homework. He was coloring in a picture of a tractor with a red crayon.

"Hey, what's up lil man," Abe said. "What ya up to?"

"Nothing. Coloring," he said assuredly.

He never looked up to break serve.

"I see, Abe said. "Nice picture you're making, what's your name?"

"Thanks. And Jailon," he said, still not looking up.

"Want me to help you stay inside the lines?" Abe said carefully.

"It's not that I can't stay in the lines. I...just...can't really 'spress myself. This pitcha too small. Need a bigger pitcha."

"Wait, that's it," Abe said.

"Like...tag you're it?!" Jailon said with excitement.

"Well, I meant what if there's a bigger picture than what has been put in front of us. You just made me realize it's okay to outgrow situations and people."

> It's okay to outgrow situations and people. Grow through what you go through.

"Don't know what you're talking about, Mister," he said before glancing over to see if Abe was paying attention.

"Tag, you're it!" Jailon said with a giggle and light tap on Abe's left arm.

"Oh no I'm not it, you're it!" Abe said as he tagged him back.

As Jailon reached across the aisle to retag him, he accidentally snapped his red crayon in half.

"Oh no, my crayon! I can't finish my pitcha now," he said with regret. "I'ma get a zero."

Abe looked over to review the damage. Yep, snapped it right down the middle.

He put his hand on his shoulder and said, "You know broken crayons still color."

"They do? How?"

"Let me show you," said Abe. With that, he grabbed the good end and began to color, holding the other stub in his left hand.

Moments later, he heard a voice call out about him:

"Last time I checked 1 + 1 was still two, gentlemen" the voice said.

It was the older, well-dressed man.

Both Abe and Jailon looked at each other with confusion as the old man reached into his pocket. He pulled out a red pocket knife and motioned for Abe to hand him the seemingly unusable crayon stub.

He began to shave the edges until the flat end became another point and second crayon. It wasn't perfect, but it was functional.

Jailon lit up with amazement.

"Wow, now I got two crayons!"

"Indeed you do, young man. Sometimes things break in two so you can get double for your trouble."

Abe reached into his bag to grab the book and began to jot the man's message down.

> Sometimes things break in two so you can get double for your trouble.

"What's that you're writing in there, young man? A journal?" the man said.

"Well, no, not exactly. My grandfather..uhh..wrote it, well kinda," Abe said shakily.

"What kind of book doesn't have words in it? Wait a minute. Are you Mackson Wright's grandboy?"

"Yes, sir. There's like one sentence on the last page, but that's it. But yeah, that was my grandfather. He passed away when I was younger." Abe shared.

"One sentence you say? Well I'll be...after all these years..." the man said, his voice trailing off.

"I can't believe the old man actually published that thing," he muttered.

"Wait, you knew him?" said Abe with confusion.

"Absolutely. He was a dear friend of mine, and now so are you. David. David K. Brooks," he said with an extended hand.

Abe shook it and introduced himself.

"Are you in school?" Mr. Brooks asked.

"Yes, I'm a senior in high school. I'm working on getting into college."

"Is that right? I'm the Dean of the business school at South University here in town. You should apply," Mr. Brooks said with encouragement.

"I'll think about it. What do I have to do?" Abe asked.

"Just email me a personal statement about your views on life, and we'll go from there."

"Okay, but what do I write about?" Abe inquired.

"More than your grandfather did for starters," he said with a laugh. "But you're smart; it'll come to you. Just something you have learned about life and how you see the world," said Dean Brooks.

"That's it?" he asked in disbelief.

"That's it," said Dean Brooks.

"I'll work on it tonight!" Abe said with excitement as he gathered his things. Ms. Gurt was approaching his stop and staring at him through her overhead mirror.

"Never know who you're gonna meet on Ms. Gurt's bus. Hay! You be good now, ya hear?" said Ms. Gurt with a wink.

Still with his notebook in hand, Abe opened to an empty page and made a new entry.

> Do not neglect to show hospitality to strangers, for many have entertained angels unawares.
>
> Hebrews 13:2

CHAPTER 12

The rest of the day was rather uneventful compared to what Abe had experienced that morning.

He couldn't wait to get home and share his experience on the bus with his parents.

Who knew a broken crayon could unite three completely different people? He began to reflect on the only words he found in the empty book by his grandfather.

> *Everything I know about life is captured in the preceding pages.*
> – FRED M. WRIGHT

"I get it now, grandpa," Abe said to himself. "We truly don't know what the story of our lives will be, but we add new entries, characters, and experiences to it every single day."

Abe walked into his house later that evening and greeted his parents. Mom was in the kitchen, and Pops was in the living room watching COPS as usual.

They both turned around as he entered to ask him how his day had gone, and Abe immediately began to describe the little boy and professor he'd met earlier that day.

Abe continued, "And the professor guy said he's going to help me get into college here at South University, too! I still cannot believe how nice he was—treated me like one of his own."

"Wait, do you remember what his name was? Did he give you a card?"

"Uh, I think his name was Brooks or something?"

"Did he carry a pocket knife, by chance?" his Pops asked.

"Wait, how did you know that? I haven't even told that part of the story yet."

Abe's parents looked at each other and smiled.

Abe's mom walked and grabbed his grandfather's book. She could tell by the bend in the spine that he had been putting it to good use.

She opened it to the second page, and motioned for Abe to come and take a look.

Directly under author Fred M. Wright's name read:

Edited by David K. Brooks

"No way," Abe mouthed in his disbelief. "But how did he edit a book with only one sentence in it? Doesn't make sense."

Abe's mom looked over at his dad.

"Remember that pocket knife I mentioned, son?" his dad started.

"Yeah, he used it to carve a tip into the little boy's broken crayon, so he could keep coloring. But I didn't even tell you abou—"

"You didn't have to. That's exactly what he did for your grandfather over forty years ago," Pops said as he rose and walked to look out the window.

"He carved the very pencil your grandfather used to write that sentence in the original manuscript. I reckon he used that same pocket knife, a red one, eh?"

Abe nodded in disbelief.

"That old man is still cuttin' up," Pops dad-joked.

They all laughed.

"Well, what he did say about college, dear," said Mom, reeling everyone back in.

"Oh he just said to type up a personal statement and email it to him," said Abe.

"Well, I don't hear no typewriter dinging," said Pops with conviction.

"No one uses those things anymore, Dad, but I'm on it. I now know exactly what I'm going to write about."

Abe began to type his personal statement to Dean Brooks.

Title: Broken Crayons Still Color

Albert Einstein once said:

"Live life to the fullest. You have to color outside the lines once in a while if you want to make your life a masterpiece.

Laugh some every day, keep growing, keep dreaming, keep following your heart. The important thing is not to stop questioning."

The following lines capture everything I know about life, as told by my grandfather.

The person with sight only sees a blank canvas. The person with vision sees the opportunity of a lifetime.

That's the difference.

May we always carve out some time to keep coloring outside the lines.

Sincerely,

Abe M. Wright

THE END

WILL BAGGETT

Acknowledgments

Inspiration exists, but it has to find you working.
PABLO PICASSO

As crazy as it sounds, much of what you just read actually happened. I've found that some of the most seemingly insignificant moments all work together to craft the beautiful mosaic that is your life.

I would like to thank my mom and dad, Maggie and Bill Baggett for believing in me. In their eyes, there is nothing I can't do, and it's made all the difference..

To you, the reader, thank you. People don't read like they used to, so I appreciate you taking time out of your day to give Hues of Hope a chance.

Always remember, there are no rules.

There are no limits.

Except for the ones you place on yourself.

Keep coloring outside the lines.

Will Baggett

About the Author

Will Baggett is a graduate of both the University of Mississippi and Baylor University. At the tender age of five, Will memorized an entire 90-minute movie (Street Fighter, 1994). Awestruck by the feat, it was then that his father knew something was either really wrong or really right with him. :)

Will would go on to take an early interest in theater, performing in multiple productions at his school and church in Grenada, Mississippi. He has since moved into commercial work, having appeared in national ad campaigns for T-Mobile, Coors Light, Vista Print, and Academy Sports & Outdoors.

He is a seventh-generation entrepreneur who draws much of his inspiration from his late grandfather, Reverend Fred Baggett, who began the legacy of entrepreneurship in his family. Will is regarded as one of the top up-and-coming keynote speakers in the country, leveraging his quick-wit and unique personality type to leave audiences more connected and inspired than ever before.

Share the Book

Did you enjoy Hues of Hope?

If so, please consider sharing a photo of the book with the hashtag #HuesOfHope.

If you would like to learn more about coloring outside the lines, please visit my website at www.WillBaggett.com.

I can be found on all social media platforms @OneBaggTalk.

Did you enjoy Hues of Hope?
If so, please consider sharing a photo of the book with the hashtag #HuesOfHope, and don't forget to leave a review on Amazon!

#KeepColoring

WILL BAGGETT

HUES OF HOPE

Milton Keynes UK
Ingram Content Group UK Ltd.
UKHW010924180724
445674UK00001B/6